Heidi Garrett

I Am Lily Dane

A Horrific Fairy Tale

I Am Lily Dane by Heidi Garrett
Half-Faerie Publishing

Copyright © 2015 by Heidi Garrett

Find out more about Heidi Garrett at
www.heidigwrites.blogspot.com

Cover Art by J.W.B.

Editing by Vince Dickinson
Proofreading by H. Danielle Crabtree

ISBN: 978-0-9907691-2-5

Other Books by Heidi Garrett

Sign up for Heidi's newsletter!
http://eepurl.com/wWKUj

Daughter of Light

(A Young Adult Fantasy Trilogy)

Isolt's Enchantment, A Prequel
Half Faerie, #1
Half Mortal, #2
War & Grace, #3

Once Upon a Time Today

(A Collection of Stand-Alone Modern Fairy Tale Retellings)

The Girl Who Believed in Fairy Tales: Three Short Stories
Beautiful Beautiful
Dreaming of the Sea
The Tree Hugger

In Collaboration with Billie Limpin

(A New Adult Paranormal Romance)

Cupcakes and Kisses

i

No, Lily. Not the butterflies!

Her belly curdles. The sour aftertaste ascends, surging in the back of her throat. She glances from side to side. No one is watching her: the cause of her bitter emotions. Around us, everyone is fascinated by the speckled wings of brilliant colors fluttering, flitting, flying among the zinnias and lilacs.

Only I am privy to Lily's desire to crush and dismember.

Frantic, I intensify my rebuke. *Lily Dane! They're helpless!*

She darts forward.

Helpless...

The girl never heeds my pleas. My only consolation is her target's escape. To the insect's warning system, her clumsy abruptness blares like a siren. Unfortunately, my Lily is nothing if not determined.

She registers her failure as tactical information and regroups.

The capture of a butterfly requires stealth, and perhaps numbers, to increase the odds of success.

I groan as she edges away from her parents and winds along a little-traveled dirt trail. After several turns, she smiles.

Except for seven sapphire-winged butterflies sipping from a puddle of mud, this isolated section of the butterfly habitat is empty.

Lily's tiny, controlled steps are imperceptible. Her hand swipes in the blink of an eye. Six creatures scatter.

With her fist deep in the pocket of her Juicy Couture velour hoody, Lily crushes the poor insect with nimble fingers.

When Spencer and Blair Dane find her, their nine-year-old daughter's face beams.

§§§

When I found myself bound to Lily Dane in the cosmic ethers where shadows and souls unite, I cried out for a liberty that could never be granted. My repulsion—born from the most elemental substances comprising our forms—persisted throughout our shared life in the womb and beyond.

Lily was a monster from the moment of conception. Not a blood-sucking, razor-toothed, gut-you-with-her-claws monster. No, she was a glacial, psychological predator.

Imagine yourself naked and defenseless in the dead of winter's brutal snow, without garments or heat, and how the pervasive chill numbs and paralyzes before it kills you without a word. Then imagine this scene infinite; your existence upon the frigid spiritual tundra extends days, weeks, years, with no relief on the horizon. Death's embrace begins to appeal, a mirage of warmth.

It makes sense—the obsession that ending Lily's life would become for me. Impotence only fueled my preoccupation. But I'm getting ahead of myself. Allow me to start from the beginning, with Lily's parents.

Spencer and Blair Dane were united in unholy matrimony for the sole purpose of accelerating their social ascension. A hedge fund manager, Spencer appreciated his wife's degree in Art History. She appeared cultivated while offering zero risk of professional competition. Theirs was a marriage of clarity; neither love nor affection complicated the emotional wasteland of their union.

However, after a particularly icy patch, Blair had occasion to view the film *The War of the Roses*. It was a random act—she considered all commercial entertainment lowbrow—which she indulged in on a whim after a few too many glasses of Pinot Noir while Spencer was away on a business trip. The undignified spectacle of the dissolution of the Rose marriage seized Blair's imagination with a premonitory grip. The following morning in yoga class, she continued to dwell on the movie's most disturbing scenes. The message became more personalized.

The universe (she went to Wellesley and didn't believe in God or god) (please!) had provided her with a clear and potent glimpse of the future were she to divorce her charming, arrogant, and manipulative husband.

The message: There could be no recovery from such an act for Blair Dane.

However, this insight did nothing to repair the Grand Canyon-sized gash in the Dane marriage.

She studied the tabloids for solutions. The images of taut, glowing mothers contradicted Blair's view of childbearing as the most direct route to mar her perfect, if frosty, figure. Stars were bouncing back after giving birth. Many looked even better than before.

If nothing else, Blair was strategic. Photoshop was considered as a cofactor in the matrix of her calculations. She couldn't expect to look as perfect as the glossy pictures, but better a few stretch marks than death by chandelier.

Spencer was intrigued.

Blair could almost hear the gears in his brain whir when she proposed the superglue that would hold their arctic union together.

A child.

Her husband favored all things that gave him an edge. Blair would artfully arrange the deal-enhancing family photo spreads on his massive mahogany desk herself.

When she became pregnant with a girl, they agreed on the name Lily. Blair interpreted this minor accord as another direct message from the universe: Your daughter, Lily Dane, will be your savior.

This is where I entered the picture, condemned by fate to be the deified Lily's shadow for the duration of my existence.

§§§

Being a shadow is not a bad thing per se. Although considered dark, we travel light. Among other things, we serve as a reservoir for non-matter imbalances which can't be rectified instantaneously in time and space by our host. Think of us as the middleman between matter and energy, the physical and metaphysical. A receptacle for psychic backwash and whatever unconscious debris the host has yet to claim.

Being the average person's shadow is not all that arduous a task. It requires mastering a few basic skills: fidelity, agility, and perseverance.

Sadly, Lily failed to inspire a single one of these traits in me. Life spent trapped in a wire cage which allowed space for form but none for movement couldn't have been worse.

Some things are born malformed. Lily and I were among those freaks of nature. You've heard of *Beauty and the Beast*? Well, my Lily was the most beautiful beast. Honey-colored hair with peachy, glowing skin, morning glory blue eyes, and graceful, willowy limbs harbored a ravenous, compulsive, scavenging nature—devouring yet vacuous.

As her shadow, I was supposed to be the dark to her light. But her light was like a solar flare, pulsing with radiation that sickened and weakened living things. Despite her namesake, even flowers shriveled when she came near.

I did my best to keep my distance, dutifully standing behind her, off to the side or beneath her. But her light was so bright it robbed me of my identity. Even when the sun was highest in the sky, I wavered, barely visible.

I endured it all in silence.

For years, when she slept at night, nestled in 400 count sheets, I imagined a life separate from her.

Fantasizing was the one thing that allowed me to face each morning when Lily sprang from her bed and dragged me in her cruel wake.

§§§

In the Dane backyard, Blair curls up in the Roberti Rattan San Tropez Sofa while Spencer stretches the length of his muscled body upon the matching chaise.

Lily comes between them, arms spread wide, and twirls.

She doesn't just spin. Beneath her lashes, she studies her parents.

As clouds drift across the sky, the Dane parents, enthralled by their daughter's physical beauty, never notice that I'm not visible.

Lily orients her body toward her father. When she's certain her mother is watching, she waltzes to Spencer and coos in his ear as she pushes his golden hair from his forehead with tiny fingers. Basking in his undivided attention, she blesses him with her thousand-watt smile.

He's a sticky mess, melting in the palm of her hand.

Blair, ignored by her husband and daughter, shifts on the sofa and coughs. She unfolds her slim legs and taps the toe of her leather sandal against the stone paving.

When Spencer hugs his daughter, Lily squirms, wiggling from his embrace. She pivots, and her father's face falls. She skips toward her mother with arms flung wide and leans in to tap Blair's nose with her own. "You're the most beautiful mommy in the world."

Her mother's eyes shine.

Behind them, Spencer folds his arms across his chest.

Stop it! I scream.

The microscopic tilt of Lily's head convinces me she registers my plea, if only as a voice in her head. But does she stop? No, she positions herself between her parents and asks, "Who loves me the most?"

Blair and Spencer chorus, "I do."

Lily preens.

This is my charge. Her reflection in the mirror and her image in the eyes of the world consume her.

ii

Sixteen-year-old Daisy Wright shimmers through life in bright-colored tennis shoes and Salvation Army dresses, always a half-size too large. She sweeps loops of her dirty-blonde hair into a rat's nest of spirals and braids. Her cherry-vanilla lip gloss accents the natural smudges beneath her eyes and the chipped nail polish on her fingernails never matches.

Daisy's only treasure is an iPod. Between every class, the buds burrow into her ears.

Lily recognizes her classmate's messy magnetism as a look she can never pull off. Perhaps she'll eat Daisy's soul instead. "What are you singing?" she asks her classmate as they sit together in the grass cross-legged.

"Just a song I like," Daisy answers.

"I want to hear it again," Lily demands.

Please, don't be flattered, I warn the girl.

But Daisy's soft alto voice grows louder under my beautiful beast's encouragement. A few of the other students turn their heads to listen. Something akin to heartburn grips Lily's throat. She imagines damage.

After school, my beast begins her research. She'd love to trick Daisy into swallowing enough sulfuric acid to permanently scar her vocal chords, but so many questions would follow—parents, doctors, maybe even the police. Then what? Unwilling to risk a record, even one guaranteed to be expunged on her eighteenth birthday, Lily continues surfing. Her assault must be untraceable. She browses various sites: Ask.fm, Whisper, and Snapchat. Lily taps her lips as she studies her computer screen. Daisy needs a smartphone.

The following week, Lily leans against the kitchen island, picking at a plate of Blair's fresh-baked cookies. "I want to invite Daisy Wright to a sleepover this weekend. Can you call her mother and ask for me?"

"Sure, pumpkin. Oh, and your new phone came today."

"Where is it?"

"On the dining room table."

Lily grabs two cookies, swings by the dining room, and prances upstairs to her bedroom. She shrugs off her backpack and parks herself in front of her vanity mirror. As she nibbles at her afternoon snack, she talks to her reflection.

"Daisy, my dad got me a new iPhone. Do you want my old one?" Lily frowns. "What if she says no?" If she has to push too hard, even Daisy might get suspicious. Lily's gaze returns to the mirror. "Wouldn't it be cool if we could text?" She affects excitement and anticipation. When she's satisfied with her performance, she Googles wiping an iPhone clean.

The next morning, Lily waits by Daisy's locker.

Daisy's eyes widen when she sees her hovering.

"Did you finish your English homework?" Lily asks.

"Almost."

"Listening to music or something?" Lily probes.

"Uh-huh."

"I can give you the rest of the answers during study hall, if you want," Lily offers.

Daisy appears unnerved. She closes her locker. "I talked with my mom about the sleepover."

"Are you coming?"

"Why didn't you just ask me yourself?"

"Sometimes mothers feel better when another mother asks."

Daisy looks pensive.

Lily doesn't relent. "Well, are you coming?"

Daisy half-smiles. "Okay, sure."

I shudder.

Lily reaches for the girl's hand and swings it awkwardly as they walk to their next class. Throughout lunch, Daisy sings softly while Lily showers her with compliments.

Images of the poor girl drowning in a pool of false praise haunt me the rest of the day.

§§§

"Have fun," Daisy's mother says from the car before abandoning her to the Danes. She's probably impressed with the mansion and Blair's exuberant welcome.

Don't let them fool you.

Neither girl is popular, so it seems each mother is happy that her daughter has found a friend.

Daisy remains quiet and observant during dinner while Lily babbles with her parents. Spencer and Blair don't draw their silent guest out. Neither does Lily. She waits until the two girls are alone in her bedroom.

My beautiful beast runs her fingers through Daisy's multiple untamed ponytails. "Can I braid it?"

"Sure."

Lily removes the five twisties circling the crown of Daisy's head in an uneven halo before brushing out her friend's unruly waves and binding them into a thick

French braid.

Daisy is impressed.

The next morning Lily slips a golden ring with a purple gemstone into Daisy's hand.

I quake with fear for the innocent girl.

"It looks expensive," Daisy says.

Lily points to a rosewood box on her dresser. The figure of a porcelain ballerina pirouettes in its center. "My parents like to give me jewelry."

"Won't they be angry that you gave it me?"

"Seeing you wear it will make me happy. That's all I care about."

Daisy slips the ring onto her finger. A shy smile curves her lips. "It fits perfectly." She holds out her hand to admire it. "Thank you."

"I want to be your best friend," Lily says.

Although caution clouds Daisy's limpid eyes, she gingerly wraps her arms around Lily's shoulders. "Best friends," she whispers.

Lily bides her time before offering the second gift.

While she waits, my beautiful beast seeks out every opportunity to snatch small, but valuable items from her classmates, including a pair of solitaire diamond earrings, a 64-gig iPod Touch, and a Betsey Johnson coin pouch. She spends a weekend snapping pictures of the haul and uploading the images onto a fake Whisper account she's created for Daisy. The Confession: *I'm an unapologetic kleptomaniac.*

Lily's hand hovers over her mouse before uploading the final picture, one of Daisy wearing Lily's amethyst ring. Finally, she clicks *Post.*

Daisy continues to bask in Lily's fake adoration. One afternoon, she confides, "I want to play *Annie* in the school musical."

Lily nods. "You'd be so good."

"I'm afraid to try out."

"Oh, don't be."

"I never sing in front of other people. What if I freeze up?"

"You sing for me all the time."

"That's different."

Lily's heart races.

I want to crush her blood-pumping muscle in my fist.

"How is it different?" Lily asks.

Daisy curls and uncurls the hem of her dress. "You're my friend."

"And I'll help you prepare for the audition. Because that's what friends do, right?"

Daisy rubs the back of the ring Lily gave her with her thumb. "It would mean everything to me to get the part."

"I have an idea." Lily pretends to search her closet and drawers.

"What are you looking for?"

"This!" Lily holds up her old cellphone loaded with the fake Facebook and Whisper accounts she created in Daisy's name. The girl won't take it. "We can text each other." Lily catches the spark in Daisy's eyes. "Whenever you're feeling nervous about the audition, I'll pump you up."

"I can't accept this," Daisy says.

"My dad bought me a new one a few weeks ago." Lily digs through her purse with her free hand. Turning to Daisy, she holds up both phones. "See, I don't need it." Again, Lily holds out the corrupted device. "Please, I want you to have it."

Daisy's resistance crumbles. She examines the phone's screen.

Lily makes a show of programming her number into Daisy's phone, and Daisy's number into her phone, before she demonstrates the texting app. When she's finished, Daisy asks about the other icons on the screen.

"Don't worry about all that," Lily instructs. "It's just stupid stuff that comes with every phone."

The trusting girl, whose curiosity rarely extends beyond music, doesn't press.

§§§

The auditions for the school musical take place on Thursday afternoon. Daisy delivers an excellent performance. No one is surprised when she gets the part of *Annie*.

Late that afternoon, when the school's halls are empty, Lily slips the stolen contraband into Daisy's locker. Early the next morning, before erasing her cyber trail, Lily uses Daisy's fake Facebook page to post links to Daisy's fake Whisper Confession on several classmates' Facebook pages.

She departs for school energized with anticipation. When the principal's office calls Daisy from class, Lily shivers with excitement.

Despite her vehement claims of innocence, Daisy is suspended from school. A different girl is cast as *Annie*.

A few days later, a couple of plain-clothes policemen return Lily's ring. Spencer and Blair hover as the police gently question their daughter. My beautiful beast is wide-eyed and charming. The police believe her when she refutes Daisy's statement that the iPhone and amethyst ring were gifts. Although she admits to texting with the girl, Lily insists she has no idea where Daisy's phone came from. Her parents confirm the girl frequently spent the night in their home.

On the way out, the men thank Spencer for his generous annual donations to their memorial fund. After they're gone, Blair asks her daughter, "Hon, where is your old phone?"

Lily's eyes glint with hostility. "Are you accusing me of lying to the police?"

"What?" Blair backpedals. "No!"

Was she?

"I donated it to the school drive for used phones." Lily leans into her father. He throws his arm around her shoulder. "They recycle them and give them to people who need them."

Spencer grins. "She's something, isn't she?"

Blair offers a nervous laugh of agreement.

§§§

Because she's too young to be tried as an adult, and it's a first offense, Daisy Wright receives probation and community service.

Lily's disappointed the girl didn't get shipped off to juvie. She needs to up her game.

For the rest of the semester, whenever I see Daisy, alone in the cafeteria, at the edge of the schoolyard, or silent in the back of a classroom, I want to rip Lily's hair out. Smash her cupid lips. Blacken her too-blue eyes. But I'm as impotent as Daisy.

iii

Although the police believe Lily's claims of innocence, the girls in her class aren't so readily deceived. That summer, they keep their distance from my beast.

An anxious Blair fills the void with field trip after field trip: countless excursions to museums, theater matinees, sailing in the bay, mother/daughter treatments at the spa, library visits, and shopping, shopping, shopping!

It all blurs together until the morning Spencer takes the family to the local zoo.

Lily pushes through the turnstile and the air shudders. The Danes are oblivious, but as my beautiful beast's crystal-embellished Jimmy Choo flats click along the pavement, a keen wave of fear suffocates. It emanates from the cages.

Every single one of them.

With our each step forward, the blanket of unease thickens.

By the time we arrive at the monkey house, the furry little creatures leap in frantic circles through their confines.

Lily and her parents wander aimlessly from cage to cage, *oohing* and *aahing* as the poor monkeys scream and chatter their escalating apprehension.

The air crackles with the electricity of their instinctual arousal. It's music to my ears. Lily's chill beauty doesn't deceive their primal cunning.

The unsolicited corroboration engenders a sense of substance within me, as if my being is accruing density. However, when I endeavor to soothe the poor creatures, before they go mad with fear, they don't seem to hear me.

Frustrated, I compulsively repeat my message. *Hush, hush. As cruel as my Lily is, she won't harm any of you. I promise.*

Their relentless squealing continues. It's discouraging.

Imagine my surprise when the shadow of a howler monkey shrieks a raspy exclamation and detaches from its owner's material form. I've never witnessed this before. The shadow creeps along the cage's perimeter. It ambulates in Lily's direction.

I twist around her to gain a better view. What is it doing? And how has it accomplished this feat of independence?

If only I could free myself from Lily Dane!

The crowd of monkeys quiets down as the rogue shadow slinks toward the family. When it is approximately three feet from my girl, Lily's body becomes rigid.

Can she see it? Her heart races. Her mouth opens and no words come out.

The shadow crouches.

Lily tugs at her father's hand, but he misinterprets the signal as a meaningless gesture.

The shadow launches itself, the act so swift, that by the time I realize its hand-like paws are squeezing Lily's throat, it's too late.

Or is it?

Lily claws at the shadow's invisible digits. Her guttural cries rivet her parents' attention. They hasten to her aid.

"Do something!" Blair screams at Spencer.

"Lily, honey, you need to calm down. Take some deep breaths in through your nose." He demonstrates. "Exhale through your mouth."

Lily's head jerks from side to side in tiny bobs.

To Blair's and Spencer's eyes, their daughter is choking on nothing.

Emboldened, I encourage the monkey's efforts. *Squeeze harder! Crush her windpipe! Don't let go!*

Lily's death will set me free!

But the monkey's shadow exhausts itself before the deed is done. Its hands finally release Lily's neck and its long arms fall to its side. It glares at Lily, panting. Perhaps it doesn't possess the raw strength to kill a corporeal being.

The shadow's owner releases a string of hoarse gibberish and the shadow retreats, loping back to its host.

Lily is petrified.

Her parents' greet her silent stillness with palpable relief.

I attempt direct communication with the monkey's shadow. *How do you do it?*

The howler monkey barks, but its shadow remains stubbornly quiet.

The Danes hurry to the monkey house exit.

Please, help me. Tell me something! Anything!

Nothing. But now I know. Separation is possible.

§ § §

Lily's first terrifying dream arrives that night. She wakes up screeching.

Her mother and father come running, their bare feet pounding the hardwood floors. Twice in one day, unfamiliar freight has washed up on the beach of their existence, and both are profoundly puzzled.

Blair administers half a prescription sleeping pill. She urges Spencer to return to bed. "You need to sleep. I'll watch over her."

"Are you sure?"

Blair drags the antique rocking chair from the corner of Lily's room. As the rocker's gliders seesaw on the carpet, she ponders this unexpected and unwelcome juncture in her daughter's life. She's not equipped to raise an imperfect child. Although this admission rattles her, dawn finds her curled up in bed beside her daughter.

The Danes spend the next day at home, watching movies in their mini-screening room and having gourmet pizza delivered to their door. They cocoon as if shutting out the world for twenty-four hours will exorcise the aberration Lily displayed at the zoo, and erase the memory of her ear-splitting shrieks the night before.

But another night brings another nightmare.

At first, I think it's a coincidence. I'm so obsessed with

the attack at the zoo that little else registers. I replay the scene of the shadow detaching from the monkey repeatedly. My fantasies become increasingly violent until each one ends with Lily's death.

The breakthrough comes when sheer exhaustion forces me to stop my endless reenactment. That night, my beast sleeps undisturbed. It is too conspicuous, this sudden peace.

Have my murderous reveries been seeding her nightmares?

My hope is aroused.

Once my energy is replenished, I seek inspiration to test my theory. Lily has never liked spiders.

That night, after she turns out the light and dozes off, I imagine a horde of furry tarantulas filing into her room.

She moans as perspiration gathers upon her brow. *The enormous arachnids crawl up her D Porthault duvet cover.* Her hands curl into fists. *Every centimeter of her bed is covered with writhing, grasping appendages.* The sheets twist as she bucks and turns. *Several spiders breach the hem of her pajamas, then the sleeves, advancing along her bare arms and legs.*

She awakes, heart racing, eyes bulging, mouth shrieking. The shrill sound is a dissonant chord that brings her parents running.

A sense of purpose and power infuses me. I want more!

At first, every effort exhausts. But the louder and longer Lily screams, the more inspired I become. As the days pass, my deficiency proves to have an unforeseen advantage. Unpredictability is far more potent than consistency. A nightmare once or twice a week creates maximum paranoia and exhaustion. It also gives me time to replenish my energy between episodes.

I soldier on, advancing scenarios far more menacing than spiders, drawing inspiration from horror movies and news reports of unsolved crimes. Grisly murders work best.

Lily sits in a packed theater. On screen, the female lead answers her phone.

Heavy breathing.

In the audience, my beast snickers.

"Eeew!" The star ends the call. She drops the phone on the table as if it's infected. Immediately, the phone rings again.

On screen, the blonde morphs into Lily. In the theater, my beast shifts forward to the edge of her seat. The phone continues to ring. Finally, the Lily-look-alike picks it up.

"I'm watching you," a slithery male voice says.

The eyes of Lily in the audience are glued to the screen; the Lily-look-alike in the film swivels her head. Enormous plate-glass windows that preside over pitch-black views surround her. She stumbles to her feet.

The slithery voice narrates her every move.

The Lily-look-alike fumbles with her phone, ending the call again. She stabs the screen, trying to dial 9-1-1.

A deathly stillness blankets the theater. Lily twists in her burgundy velvet seat. When did everyone leave? Her heartbeat escalates. On the screen, her mirror image has succeeded in placing her emergency call.

The slithery voice answers, "I'm already here."

Ten feet away, the knob on the front door jiggles. The Lily-look-alike screams.

In the theater, a slithery voice whispers in Lily's ear, "I'm already here."

Lily opens her mouth to scream. No sound comes out. Not even a squeak. Her mouth opens and closes around silence.

Strong hands enclose her throat and squeeze.

By the end of summer, Lily fears closing her eyes.

A restful night's sleep is a thing of the past. Her mounting fatigue dampens her ability to hold sway over others.

Spencer and Blair attend fewer soirees and charity events. What would they answer when asked: How's Lily?

A wreck? Troubled? Disturbed? Paranoid? Unstable? Unbalanced?

Better to decline invitations and avoid the conversations altogether.

Finally, a desperate Blair finagles a prescription of Ambien for her daughter. The drug closes Lily's mind to my penetration. Her night terrors go into remission, and I am powerless once again.

iv

An irresistible opportunity presents itself to my beautiful beast at the beginning of her junior year. The perfect target. Lily pounces on the unsuspecting new girl, Charlene Vale.

Although she shops at Walmart (Lily's best guess) and is not a classic beauty (says Blair), Charlene enchants the boys at Dunstan High with some intangible quality oozing from within. A capacity for joy? A delight for life? Who knows? But a pack of hormonal boys always follow in the wake of Charlene's laughter.

Lily is as unnerved by her arrival as she is intrigued by the spell the young lady casts around everyone who comes near her. So when Trey Mason, the most popular boy in the eleventh grade, falls hard for Charlene, and she for him, my little beast's next project is conceived.

It begins, of course, with overtures of friendship. Lily observes her classmate in detail, noting what knock-offs she favors, what foods she eats, and how she orders her latte at Starbucks.

The needy daughter of a single, hardworking mother, Charlene gradually relaxes into the embrace of Lily's dark wings.

They make a striking pair. Where Lily is blonde and waxen, Charlene is raven and bronzed.

By midterm, the girls are inseparable.

I make various attempts to converse with Charlene's shadow. *Please, go away! Lily is dangerous! Don't trust her!*

The listless thing never responds.

Am I the only human shadow on the planet blessed with sentience?

When Charlene confides how deeply she longs to be head cheerleader, Lily's path becomes clear. She sets the stage during a Friday night sleepover.

After the pizza is delivered, Lily ushers her new BFF into the Dane screening room. While Charlene spins in circles, agog over the mini-amphitheater, Lily pulls out five worn-looking *Bring it On* DVDs. She purchased the used collection at a discount earlier that afternoon from Hastings.

"Oh my God!" Charlene squeals.

Lily blinks. "I've always loved these movies. Although I'm not very coordinated, I'd be happy to help you make the squad."

Charlene drops the DVDs and squeezes her friend. "Don't say that, Lils. I'm sure all you need is a little practice." Her deep brown eyes flash. "Let's practice together."

"Oh, I don't want to hold you back. You're probably so

far ahead of me, I'll never catch up."

"There's nothing I can do that you can't learn in the next four months," Charlene assures her.

Unfortunately, truer words were never spoken.

"You really think I could make the squad too?"

"Of course, you can," Charlene cheers her BFF on.

"Well, if you promise to help."

"We can win together!"

The girls stay up all night, watching the movies. The next afternoon they hit the Dane lawn for their first practice session. Charlene pours every ounce of joy and enthusiasm into helping Lily learn the basic cheers and movements. When spring training rolls around, Lily enlists her mother as chauffeur.

"We need to make every training session scheduled," she tells Blair.

As usual, Blair clears her calendar according to her daughter's needs.

Charlene, whose mother works full time—and most days late—is so appreciative.

Lily never mentions the gymnastics classes she enrolls in after winter break, but she spends every afternoon she isn't training with Charlene at the gym, tumbling.

My beast has astutely assessed that while Charlene is pretty, magnetic, genuine, and vivacious, the execution of the more challenging acrobatic moves is beyond her. Lily never stops building her friend's confidence. "Don't let that stop you from becoming head cheerleader and partner to Trey's football team captain," she encourages her BFF.

The day Lily perfects her *round off back handspring back tuck*, Spencer and Blair take their daughter out to dinner at the most expensive restaurant in town. That night, Lily turns off her phone.

The next morning, Charlene asks, "Where were you last night?"

Lily acts bewildered. "Huh?"

"I called and texted."

My beast holds up her hands. "My mom and dad took my phone."

"What? No way! Your mom is always so cool!"

"She's concerned all this cheerleading practice is taking away from my scholastics."

"Really?"

Lily nods.

"But she drives us to the all practices herself."

"She's okay if I try out, she just doesn't want me to let my grades slip."

"Didn't you get straight As last semester?"

"Yeah, but they expect me to get them every semester. And Monday I got a C on my algebra test," Lily lies.

Charlene will never compare notes. Academics aren't on her radar. She only exists for cheerleading and Trey Mason. "Ouch," she commiserates.

"The worst is she's refusing to drive us to any more cheerleading practices until my grades come back up."

Panic flits across Charlene's face. "But tryouts are in two weeks! We can't miss those sessions."

"And my next algebra test isn't until the following Monday. Sucks! I tried to explain it to her, but she won't budge. No more cheerleading practice until my grades come back up."

Wetness sparkle in the corner of Charlene's eyes.

Lily knows her friend has no other transportation to the sessions being held at different girls' homes around town.

"That's such a bummer." Charlene brushes her eyes before throwing her arms around her BFF. "I'll just practice by myself at home. You do the same."

"Promise." Lily hugs her friend back.

§ § §

"Charlene can't make practice today," Lily tells Blair after school.

"No?"

"She caught some awful bug and had to go home early."

Blair presses her palm against her daughter's forehead. "I hope it's not contagious."

"I'm fine."

"Okay. Well, keep your distance until she's recovered. I can't afford to catch something right now either."

"I told her to let me know as soon as she's feeling

better."

Blair hugs her daughter tight. "You're such a smart girl, so level-headed. It makes me proud." She smiles over Lily's shoulder. Blair's own perky encouragement quells her troubling suspicion that something is deeply awry with her daughter.

The next day at school, Charlene seems distant.

Lily corners her after third period. "Is everything all right?"

"I thought you couldn't make practice, but Susie said you were there yesterday afternoon. What gives?"

"Wow. Are you accusing me of lying?"

"I don't know. You said your mother wasn't going to take you to practice until after your next math test. Which, by the way, is after tryouts."

Lily holds up her phone. "You didn't get my text?"

"No!" Charlene digs around in her bag. She pulls out her phone and thumbs through her text messages. "Nothing."

Lily leans her back against the lockers. "Weird. I

wondered why I didn't hear from you. Mom felt guilty at the last minute and caved."

Charlene's face flickers between confusion and hope. "Does that mean we can make the session today?"

"Maybe. I hope so. But my mother's been moody lately. One minute, she's fine, and the next minute, she's all psycho. I think she's going through menopause or something."

Over the next ten days, my beautiful beast finesses the art of evasion, and Charlene misses every single cheer practice.

The Friday of tryouts, Charlene is a wreck. Tearful, insecure, and full of self-doubt, while my Lily is poised, calm, and self-assured.

Lily holds her BFF's hand while they sit in the front row of the auditorium, watching the other candidates perform. When they're backstage, Lily hugs Charlene tight. "Go get 'em!" She makes an enthusiastic display of rooting for her friend from the wings.

Charlene's performance is solid but not inspired.

Lily congratulates her before she steps into the limelight herself. When she finishes her routine with a perfect *round off back handspring back tuck*, she doesn't miss Charlene's gaping mouth in the audience.

Her friend is diffident when Lily catches up with her.

The next day, Charlene gives Lily a cool hug after the members of the squad are announced during the last period over the school PA.

"You seem a little bummed," Lily says.

Charlene shakes her head, but she can't look Lily in the eye. "You did great. You deserve to be on the squad, and head cheerleader. Congratulations." She stares at the linoleum floor marked with sneaker treads.

Lily squeals, "I still can't believe it!" It's the last day of school. She has all summer to prepare her assault on Charlene's relationship with Trey.

§§§

Lily and Charlene don't spend much time together over the summer break.

At cheer camp, my loathing of Lily metastasizes as she

dominates the other campers. My determination to find some way to stop her grows.

Imagine my elation when, one morning while the girls stretch, I refuse to match my arms with my host's. I simply clamp them by my side as Lily waves her pale limbs in the air, twirling them left, then right, and finally sweeping them to the ground.

Success!

Managing my legs proves more challenging. When Lily kicks and squats, my limbs follow suit. I don't allow the defeat to make me despondent. If I can free my arms and hands, the day will come when I can separate my legs and feet too! Then I'll be able to strangle my little beast in her sleep. Although she's no longer little, having achieved a willowy 5'8".

I soon discover that initiating movement is not the same as resisting it. My frustration with my impotence remains boundless.

There has to be something that I, the witness to Lily's every crime, can do. Some means for me to achieve justice. A method to end her senseless destruction of those who possess souls more attractive than hers.

Who am I kidding? Lily's soul is a plague. There is nothing attractive about it.

v

On the first day of their senior year, Lily spies Trey hanging on Charlene's locker. She struts over, interrupts their conversation, and showers her former BFF with a fake, "Hi! How was your summer?" Then she grabs Trey by the arm and pulls him away on the pretext that Mr. Sumner, the football coach, needs to speak with them.

However, the coach isn't in his office and can't be located—anywhere. What a surprise!

Finding themselves alone in a cavernous stairwell, Lily

gazes into Trey's hazel eyes with her cool blues. She brushes a stray lock of hair from his forehead. "Sorry, I must have misunderstood what time coach wanted to meet." Lily allows her hand to rest on Trey's shoulder.

He gulps. "I guess we should get to class."

Lily stands on her tiptoes and presses her lips against his.

His eyes widen in shock.

"I've always wanted to do that." She curls her hand around Trey's neck and gently pulls his face to hers. Then she kisses him in earnest. When he fumbles for her breasts, she doesn't stop him right away. But once his arousal is apparent, she pulls back. "Oh my God! I'm so sorry. Please, don't tell Char. She'll hate me."

Trey's hands retreat to Lily's waist. "Oh, your secret is safe with me."

Lily grins. This is going better than she hoped. She tilts her head. "Does that mean we can do this again?"

"Oh, definitely," Trey says.

How can Charlene Vale love this boy?

"So you liked it?" my beast asks.

"I did." Trey holds her gaze as his hands travel from her waist to the hem of her crop top.

She holds her breath when his fingers find skin, and she doesn't stop him when his fingers move upward to push inside the cups of her Victoria's Secret demi-bra to squeeze her nipples. She almost faints with lust.

Oh, something she can feel!

She thrusts her hips toward his as a moan escapes her lips. Although she isn't sexually experienced, she understands that boys prefer girls who don't hold back.

"You like that?" Trey's breathy question makes her reel.

"Mmmhmm," she murmurs.

The bell rings, shattering their interlude.

Trey slips his hands out from beneath her shirt. He runs his tongue across his lower lip. "Text you later?"

"Sure."

§ § §

I become more determined than ever to put a stop to her.

However, I still can't puff enough air to alter the path of a feather. This time, I don't allow my failures to derail me. I vow to find a way.

Every sordid encounter Lily has with Trey increases my determination to end her predation of these girls who are more vital and alive than she is; girls who don't need to rely on destruction as shock therapy to jolt their inner corpses.

A few weeks before winter break, Lily and Char are in the girls' bathroom, applying lip gloss and arranging their hair, when Lily notes the tears melting down Charlene's cheeks.

"What's wrong?" She actually sounds concerned.

Char shakes her head.

Lily deposits her jar of Bobbi Brown lip balm into her Luis Vuitton Patchwork purse (there are only twenty-four in existence!) and turns toward Char. Lily squeezes her ex-best friend's shoulder.

Char's chest caves, and she breaks down into heaving sobs.

Lily goes for a tissue, one of the few decent things she's ever done. "Char, what is it?"

Charlene peeks under the stalls to make sure no one is with them before she whispers, "I'm pregnant."

Lily is stunned. When her trysts with Trey had advanced from singles to home runs, they'd always used protection. "You're not on the pill?"

Charlene puffs her chipmunk cheeks. "I forget."

"Oh," is all Lily can muster. Abandon is for sexual gymnastics, not for birth control. "Does Trey know?" He hasn't mentioned it to Lily.

"No. And I can't tell him. I can't ruin his life."

Lily is hit with a rush of adrenaline as she contemplates possible outcomes. Will it be worse for Char if she and Trey have a shotgun wedding and become low-rent teen parents? Or would the damage be greater if Char has an abortion? Lily's mind advances at the speed of light. How to inflict the deepest wound? She quickly decides that whatever happens, Char needs to confide in Trey. She studies the girl.

Trey doesn't lack sexual prowess. In fact, Lily is addicted to his craving for pushing the erotic envelope. But Lily has no illusions; Trey is a complete and total asshole. He'll never stand by Charlene and his unborn child. At best, he'll offer to pay for the abortion.

"You have to tell him," Lily says.

"I know." Charlene sniffles. "Do you think he'll hate me?"

"Oh no," Lily says. "He loves you. He'll want you to have the baby."

"You think so?"

"Do you want to have the baby?"

Charlene angles her body so she can look at herself in the mirror. Lily repositions herself beside her. Their eyes meet in the mirror.

"I'm not sure if I'm ready," Charlene admits.

Lily looks at Char, but I stare straight ahead, directly into the mirror, refusing to be part of my beast's cruel machinations. That's when I see myself! My own form, distinct from Lily's! I look just like her! Except, I'm brunette and my eyes are the deepest shade of brown. I scream! Neither girl hears me, but I see my lips move. I flatten them together. I part them and form an O. I close and open my eyes then wink. First my left eye then my right.

Which leads to the decisive discovery: My desire to aid Lily's victims strengthens me. My affection for Charlene has been the fuel to push my will into the corporeal plane.

I smile at myself in the mirror. Victory!

Whatever further damage Lily Dane wreaks upon Charlene Vale, she will pay for it. I will free myself from my ball-and-chain and make sure of it!

§§§

A few weeks later, Trey guides Lily's head. She doesn't resist, only performs as he indicates, and listens while he unloads his stress over Charlene's pregnancy.

After he unloads his physical emission, Lily carefully wipes her lips. "What are you going to do?"

"You want to go steady?" Trey asks.

"Go steady?" Lily is in shock. Shock that has nothing to

do with Charlene Vale. Trey is a means to an end, he was never meant to be a happily ever after himself.

He pulls Lily into his lap. "We've got something special, don't you think?" He pushes her naked legs wide and dives his hand between them.

She arches her back.

Trey's lips round on her nipple before biting, just hard enough to hurt so good.

Lily lets go long enough to experience an authentic orgasm. However, as soon as the glow lifts, her mind races.

Charlene has no idea her best friend and boyfriend are doing it behind her back—and with increasing frequency.

Lily recalls something Charlene told her: "He hasn't touched me since I told him that I was pregnant."

"How do you think making our relationship public will affect Charlene?" Lily asks.

Trey brushes the tip of her nose with his index finger. "You're always putting others first."

Gag me.

Lily shrugs. "She's my best friend."

"I don't love her," he says.

"What about the baby?"

"I told her to get an abortion."

"What did she say?"

"Boohoo-ed. Then she told me how much she loved me and how cute our baby would be. All that crap."

Lily nods. Charlene has told her all of this, but she wants to hear him confirm it.

"Listen, my old man is willing to pull whatever strings it takes to get me out of this mess. Understand?"

She understands completely.

That night Lily yells at Char, "You can't just give up! Not if you really love him." She knows Char does. "Your baby needs its father. He has to come around!" Right to Life pamphlets are spread on the bed between them. Lily picks one up. "It's your responsibility as the baby's mother to save its life. Abortion is murder."

"But Trey has cut me off completely." Char breaks down. "He won't take my calls. He doesn't answer my texts. I think he's blocked my number."

"You need to go to his house. You need to talk to his parents."

"What am I going to say?"

"Tell them—" She stops to think. "Tell them—" She thumbs through the pamphlet in her hand. "Tell them this is their grandchild, and you'll sue Trey for child support if you have to."

"I don't know." Charlene stares out Lily's bedroom window. "Maybe I should just get the abortion."

"I thought you didn't want an abortion."

"I don't, but I don't think I'm strong enough to raise a child by myself."

"You shouldn't have to!"

"I can't make him love me, or this baby."

"He's just scared."

"I think it's more than that."

Lily's shoulders stiffen. "What do you mean?"

"I think he's seeing someone else."

"Why do you think that?"

"He likes having a girlfriend."

More like a semen receptacle.

"Don't give up," Lily pushes.

I can't bear any more of her cruel ruse. I channel all of my compassion for Charlene into my hands. I push with every ounce of my consciousness and raise my hands. My shadow hands are lifting up! I guide them to Lily's throat and squeeze!

She chokes as she claws at my iron grip. Just like the howler monkey!

Charlene stares with her mouth agape.

It's fleeting, but I will never forget the sensation of compressing the girl's dove-white neck. It invigorates my dream of ending Lily's life. Of late, my beast has become careless with her sleeping pills. She's vulnerable. The idea of simultaneously penetrating Lily's mind, while enacting my will into the material plane titillates me.

It holds such possibility.

vi

Charlene's ambivalence about abortion delays her from taking action. She prefers running her hands over the swell in her belly to scheduling an appointment with Planned Parenthood. But it is the riffle of tiny kicks that change her mind. She can't kill her child.

And though she shies away from Lily's advice to go to Trey's parents, she still hopes he'll come around.

§§§

Char sprawls across Lily's bed. "I'm not sure I want to go

to the party."

Lily flounces down beside her. "Oh, come on."

Char points to her tummy. "I can't drink alcohol. What am I going to do when everyone else gets wasted?"

It's the first Friday night of winter break.

Lily smooths Char's riot of sable hair. "I'll ride with you and find another way home, or call my mom. That way you can leave early if you want."

Char hesitates, but then says, "Oh, all right."

Lily is pissed at Charlene for not mounting a stronger campaign on behalf of her unborn child with its father and his family. Not that Lily has a whiff of concern for the rights of the mother or the child. It's more that Char has had the audacity to ignore her advice and witlessly evade her manipulation.

Her goal is to break Charlene. How can that happen if the girl comes to terms with her situation and lets Trey off the hook?

On the way to the party, neither girl says much. The street is already packed with cars. Char has to park the old

Toyota her mother bought her last summer a few blocks away. When Lily jumps out, Char hesitates.

What is going on in her mind?

Lily circles around to the driver's side. When Char rolls down the window, I have a dark premonition. Something terrible is going to happen if Char gets out of her car.

It has been a long time since I've tried to make contact with another person's shadow, but out of desperation, I make a frantic attempt to connect with Char's.

As usual, I receive no response. My panic escalates as Lily coaxes Char to come inside.

As we walk across the threshold, loud music, loud voices, and loud laughter assault our ears.

Lily cuts through the crowd with precision. She's searching for Trey. She doesn't see him before he grabs her around the waist and plants a sloppy kiss on her lips.

He's already drunk. He smashes Lily against his chest and begins to openly fondle her.

Char stands ten inches away, paralyzed.

Lily smiles.

In those few seconds, everything comes together for Char: her boyfriend's infidelity, his new girlfriend, Lily's insistence that Char demand Trey throw his desired future aside to play house with her. Everything has been a lie.

"What the fuck is wrong with you?" Charlene shouts.

Trey finally notices her standing there. "You need to get that taken care of." He jabs a finger toward Charlene's belly. "Your hormones are out of control."

"I'm not talking to you," Char spits the words out. Her glare never leaves Lily's face.

My beast winks. "It doesn't mean anything, Char."

Trey is now behind Lily, pressing his body against hers, and running his chin over the top of her head.

Char's eyes narrow, her brow furrows. "You set this whole thing up. This is what you've wanted all along. To humiliate me, ruin me. Why?"

"Because I can."

Char stabs the space between them with her index finger. "Rot in hell, Lily Dane!" The agony of the moment fills her eyes. She fights her way through the circle of inebriated students who have packed in around the trio.

Lily laughs. It's a carefree, satisfied utterance.

Revulsion overtakes me. It collides with the seismic need to comfort Char. Waves of horror crash into waves of compassion, and a volcanic potency erupts within me.

I find myself slicing through the crowd and racing out the door, completely unencumbered by Lily. I don't have time to appreciate what I've accomplished, because it's too late. Char's car disappears into the night before I can reach the curb.

The next day, the headline in the town's newspaper rocks the entire community: **Local student, unborn child die in collision with tree**.

I spend my first day free of Lily pacing beneath the fatal oak. I'll never be her prisoner again. But Charlene Vale has died, humiliated and broken.

I'm determined Lily Dane will die, even if it's the only thing I ever achieve.

§§§

For the next few weeks, I remain completely separate from Lily.

I make my home beneath the oak, curling up next to the shrine of gifts left in memory of Charlene and her unborn child. I spend the majority of each day focusing on manipulating inanimate objects. I start with barely visible pebbles, move up to twigs, and when I become adept, advance to tidying up the memorial by setting fallen candles, teddy bears, and framed photos aright, and clearing away debris, leaves, and trash that collect among the treasures.

All the while, I ponder how to best my Lily. The nightmares I seeded were child's play and choking her that single time had little effect. I begin to wonder: Can I induce Lily to inflict harm upon herself?

On a cool, crisp, clear night, I'm ready to make my first attempt. I mosey over to the Dane mansion and climb the tree outside Lily's bedroom window. I'm relieved to find it open, only the screen blocking my progress. I kick that in.

Lily shifts beneath her electric blanket.

I join her beneath the covers.

Despite the wintery temperature, her body burns as if she's a spawn of hell. She's like a reptile.

The second our forms reattach, a sense of being suffocated overwhelms me. Existing as a discrete entity has altered me. Being attached to Lily feels wrong. What if I'm trapped and can never free myself again? I spend the next few minutes struggling to recreate the distance between us.

Finally, our entities pop apart, like a cork exiting a bottle of champagne.

Never again will I risk rejoining with Lily.

I rise from the bed and walk around her room, gathering my energy and concentration. When I catch a glimmer of myself in the mirror, I freeze. There I stand again, a dark-haired, dark-eyed replication of Lily. I advance to the mirror and gaze at my reflection.

How is this miracle possible when no one else can see

me? I graze my cheek with my fingers and feel the sensation.

Lily tosses and turns behind me.

I bend over her restless form, placing one hand on either side of her, and whisper into her ear, "Rise, rise, rise."

Lily's hand flails.

I easily dodge her fist. "Rise, but don't wake," I coax.

Her head rolls from side to side.

"Good, you can hear me. Now, rise from your bed, Lily Dane, and walk," I coo.

Her torso shoots up, and I step back. "Come, Lily. Let's go downstairs."

She pushes aside her bedcovers and flattens her feet against the carpet. Her eyes remain closed as she responds to my promptings.

"Come, Lily."

She stands up and follows my voice.

I lead her down the long hall to the stairs.

She moves without hesitation.

I'm elated that she obeys so blindly as I lead her into the kitchen. Ah. There is the set of Wusthof knives. "Yes, my dear, sweet, Lily, take a handle, any handle."

She slides a wicked blade from its crevice.

"Yes, that's right. Now, rotate the blade toward you." I hum. It seems to soothe her and she responds more readily. "Yes, that's a clever girl. The target is the empty place in your chest, where your heart should be."

Lily nods. Is it agreement?

"Make one swift, forceful strike. Straight in."

Lily lifts the blade, the steel shines in a shaft of moonlight.

"Oh God, Lily!" Blair Dane's scream shatters the kitchen.

Fluorescent lights flicker overhead, making Lily's eyelids flutter. She loses her balance in a groggy stumble, banging her hip against the tiled island. The blade clatters to the floor.

"What are you doing?" Blair's panicked voice crowds the space.

"I don't remember coming downstairs."

Spencer, rubbing sleep from his eyes, stands next to his wife. "What is going on?"

"She tried to kill herself! She tried to commit suicide in our kitchen!" With a manic sweep of her arm, Blair gestures to the knife on the floor and the set on the counter. "Get them all out of here!"

Spencer's puzzled expression doesn't preclude him from following his wife's instructions.

Blair squeezes Lily's bicep. "We've given you everything, we've done everything for you, we've built our lives around you, and this is how you thank us? Suicide? How dare you?"

Lily whimpers. "It wasn't me."

Blair's harsh gaze searches the kitchen. "Please, Lily. No one else is here!"

"I just...I just..."

Spencer returns. "Get her sleeping pills."

Lily doesn't protest.

Blair twists the plastic cap off the bottle and shoves four

capsules at her daughter.

"That's too many," Lily says.

"I can't risk you waking up," Blair says.

"Fine," Lily grumbles as she accepts a glass of water and gulps all four pills down at once.

"What are we going to do?" Spencer asks after Lily is asleep.

Blair shakes her head. "I thought we had all this behind us."

"Apparently not." Spencer sighs.

"I don't understand what is wrong with her."

"Maybe she needs more intensive help," he says.

"What do you mean?"

"We can't risk her slicing herself up in our home."

"I know we can't!"

"Maybe it's time to consider inpatient treatment."

"Have her institutionalized? But what about school? What about her future?"

"She's not going to have a future if she kills herself. And we won't either."

"It's all because of that Charlene Vale, the pregnant girl who died. Lily tries to pretend it doesn't bother her."

"Whatever the reason, she needs to get past this."

"If we have her committed, everyone is going to talk."

Spencer pulls his wife to him and encircles her with his arms. "It'll be okay. We'll keep it quiet, and get her the best care possible. We're not equipped to handle this ourselves. She needs professional help, and I don't want her to come back here until we're sure she won't pull a stunt like this again."

Tears trickle down Blair's face, but she doesn't argue. She never wants to see her daughter with a knife in her hand again.

vii

The next afternoon, the family makes the long drive to the Careview Psychiatric Hospital for Challenged Teens. At the end of a winding road lined with sentinel cypress trees, a sleek two-story construction, more suited to a new age church than a medium-security institution for adolescents, awaits Lily Dane.

My screaming, defiant beast is dragged, then strapped to a gurney and wheeled down white halls, interrupted by painfully bright furniture.

"I don't belong here. I didn't try to kill myself. I'm not crazy," she repeats to the receptionist, the intake counselor, the orderlies, the other patients, and her parents.

Everyone ignores her.

Blair and Spencer harden themselves against their daughter's protests. Their princess has failed them. No longer a source of joy and pride, she has transformed into something dark and troublesome, a stranger they long to be rid of.

Neither parent requires a hard sell to sign the consent forms. While Blair spends a few final agitated moments with their daughter, Spencer handles the financial arrangements.

Careview is a private facility.

The best.

Expensive.

Hands entwined, Spencer and Blair exit the hospital. A fragile bond, born of mutual disappointment and guilt, deepens over their shared failure. Ironic that their daughter's fall humanizes them.

Sensing the climax is near, I remain at Careview.

§§§

A young man sidles up to Lily in the corridor. "What are you in for?"

"They think I tried to kill myself with a kitchen knife."

"Did you?"

"Why would I try to kill myself? That's just stupid."

"You don't look so good," he says.

"It's all the drugs. I've never taken so many pills in my life."

He nods. "You're pretty."

She examines him with more care and smiles. "You're not half bad yourself. What are you in for?"

"I write a blog from the perspective of a serial killer, *Killing Frenzy*. Very detailed. The members of the gated community where my dad and stepmother live didn't appreciate the blog's popularity. Neither did the local police. My stepmother didn't appreciate the neighbors' or the police's harassment. When I refused to stop posting, my dad dumped me in here."

Lily takes a couple of steps back. "You're still writing it?"

"My fans will be dying to hear from me when I get out." He laughs at his joke.

"Whatever." She dodges around him.

His arms are long. He grabs a lock of her hair. "This would make a great trophy."

Lily jerks her head. "You obviously belong here," she says between clenched teeth.

His hand is behind her neck before she can react. He forces her face close to his. "All the victims on my blog are based on real people. The first one was a girl down the street. Her parents weren't pleased when I made her an internet star."

Lily's pulse pounds. She struggles to free herself.

"What's wrong?" he asks. "I could make you a star too."

"Get your hands off me."

He tightens his grip on the back her neck.

Lily's eyes widen.

She swings her leg out to kick him, but he shoves her to the side and she misses.

He pushes her up against the wall.

"Get off me!" she yells.

An orderly rounds the corner, and he releases her. "My name is Brian, by the way." He holds out his hand as if he wants her to shake it. "I just want to get to know you better."

She hurries past him.

When Lily reaches her barren room, she throws herself on the spartan bed and shivers. After her arms and legs stop trembling, she stands up to pace. "He just physically assaulted me," she mumbles to herself. "But who is going to believe me? No one believes I didn't try to kill myself." She hugs herself. "This is so fucked up." She tiptoes to the door, cracks it, and peeks out. A few people walk through the halls. Relieved to see them, Lily steps out of her room.

She heads to the nurse's station. "I need to make a

phone call."

The nurse raises her head. "You haven't earned that privilege yet, Lily."

This place is going to drive her insane! She slaps her palm against the counter.

The nurse's shoulders tense with wariness. "Lily, calm down."

"I just need to make one phone call."

"The rules are clear. Making phone calls is a privilege you earn."

Lily hunches over the counter. "Do you know Brian?"

The nurse steeples her fingers. "I do."

"He's going to kill me."

The nurse stands up and rounds her desk. "He suffers from delusions."

"I'm terrified of him."

"I'll make a note in your file."

"You need to do something to protect me."

"Did he hurt you?"

"He grabbed me by the neck!"

"Lily, you need to calm down."

"Don't tell me to calm down!"

"Lily—"

"He fucking grabbed me by the neck and threatened my life!"

"Lily, take some deep breaths. What exactly did he say?"

"He told me about his blog. He wanted to know my name." Even Lily knows how lame and paranoid she sounds.

The nurse punches some buttons on the intercom. "Code 24 at the front desk."

"God!" Lily shouts. "You're just going to drug me. That's your answer to everything here. Just give me another fucking pill."

She slides down the wall and waits for the orderlies to come. When they thrust the tiny paper cup and a small plastic glass of water at her, she takes her medication.

Lily wakes up in her bed in the middle of the night, her stomach growling. She's missed dinner. She stares at the blank walls.

She's alone.

Her parents have abandoned her.

She has no friends.

Zero.

No one.

§§§

I watch Lily from a distance. She sits at a table in the common room, pretending to read. Brian enters and I stand straighter. He lowers himself into a chair across from her. She ignores him.

"Are you aware that you don't have a shadow?" he asks.

His statement rivets my attention.

Lily presses her lips into a thin, hard line.

"I've never seen that before," he continues.

She slams her book. "You belong here," Lily says. "I don't."

Brian raises his hands, palms up, facing her. "We got off on the wrong foot." He lowers his elbows to the table. "I've been told I can be too aggressive."

"You needed someone to enlighten you?"

"I only model victims on girls who are really hot."

"Is that supposed to be a compliment?"

"Isn't it?"

Lily snorts. "You really have all the doctors and nurses fooled, don't you? They think you're delusional. You're just some *Dexter* fan who can't differentiate between fantasy and reality. But you don't have me fooled." She sniffs. "I can smell the rot on you. So listen up." She pushes her chair away from the table. "Don't imagine me as one of your victims, because if you ever touch me again, I'm going to fucking kill you." She nods to the attendant across the room. "And they'll just chalk it up to the escalation of my psychopathy," she snarls.

"Touché."

"You are nuts!"

"And you don't have a shadow, Lily Dane."

"How in the fuck do you know my name?"

"As you so astutely pointed out, I've got most of the worker bees at Careview wrapped around my finger." He wags his pinky as Lily fumes. "One of the nurse's aides was very forthcoming when I asked a few questions about the new girl."

"How dare you! I am none of your business."

"But no one else in Careview is as compelling a subject as you." He waves his arm. "Do you see that?"

"What?"

"Watch my shadow." He waves his arm again. "Now you do it."

"No."

"Then you already know you don't have a shadow."

She hisses, "You are crazy."

"Humor me." Brian stretches his long arm across the table.

She twists farther out of his reach, the legs of her chair squeaking on the parquet floor. "Don't touch me. Ever."

"All right. All right." He chews on his lower lip. "But I've been trying to figure out why you don't have one." Eager to prove him wrong, she waves her arm in the air. Nothing. The table's surface remains a blank slate. Lily shifts in her seat. She waves her arm again. Still nothing. She alters the angle of her torso. No shadow. "How is that even possible?" Was she born this way? Is that what is wrong with her? Because as much as she hates to admit it, every day Lily remains at Careview, it becomes harder and harder for her to ignore the nagging idea that there is something troubling about her personality. But not having a shadow? She gazes at Brian, who quirks one eyebrow.

No one else has ever noticed. She has never noticed. Lily slides her chair back to the table and sits down sideways. "Okay, so I don't have a shadow."

"Maybe that's why you're here," Brian says in a loud whisper.

Lily tries to recall the last time she saw me. She can't remember. It's beyond strange. She folds her arms across her chest and rubs her elbows.

"I noticed it the first time I saw you, and I've given it a lot of thought," Brian says.

She doesn't like to imagine him giving any part of her a

lot of thought.

"I think your shadow abandoned you. I think it didn't like you. I think it wanted to get away from you."

By now, I've crept closer. How has he figured it out?

She hunches over, repositioning her forearms on her knees. "Shadows can't just leave because they want to."

"And yet, yours is MIA." He spreads his hands and looks from side to side.

Lily rearranges herself in her seat again. Every time she moves, she scans the floor for my presence. But as long as we're separate, I'm invisible to the naked eye. She can't see me, only a few feet away. Neither can Brian.

"It's really gone," he confirms.

"You don't know whether or not I ever had one. Maybe I was born without one. Maybe I'm a goddamned saint or something."

"I don't think so."

"And why is that?"

"Because you're not just mean to me, you're mean to everyone here."

"Well, at least I'm not a wannabe serial killer," she hisses.

"Maybe body counts aren't your thing."

"And what in the hell is that supposed to mean, smart-ass?"

"Maybe you just murder people's spirits."

Lily's eyes widen. "I don't know what the hell you're talking about."

Brian smirks. "I think you know exactly what I'm talking about. Maybe your shadow got disgusted with you." He glances around to ensure no one is in earshot. "Maybe your *shadow* tried to kill you."

Lily blinks several times. "I'm not going to listen to any more of your crap."

Brian shrugs. "You not having a shadow isn't *my* crap."

§ § §

Lily spends the rest of the afternoon in the tiny enclosed courtyard, moving in the sunlight, craning her head behind her, searching for me.

That night she lies in bed with her eyes wide open,

considering her situation.

The next morning, Brian joins her at breakfast. Lily doesn't tell him to go sit somewhere else.

"Maybe I never had a shadow," Lily muses as she digs channels through her cold, lumpy oatmeal with a plastic spoon. "I'm just some freak of nature."

"Oh, you're a freak of nature all right," Brian says. "Look, I'm a psychopath. I don't lie to myself and then try to believe otherwise. But I've got a fucking shadow."

"Are you trying to say that by not having a shadow, I'm worse than a murderous fetishist like you?"

"Something like that."

"Well, good morning to you too, Mr. Sunshine."

Brian laughs.

"What is so goddamned funny?"

"The only thing that matters to you is that no one but me has ever noticed that you don't have a shadow."

"Don't you think that's weird?"

"That no one pays much attention to you? Why would they?"

Lily stiffens.

"I mean you're beautiful, gorgeous. But you're cold and heartless."

"You don't know me."

"I recognize my own kind. Of all the psychopaths I've met, you're the emptiest."

"Shut up."

"Pushed a button? I don't have to know you when I can feel you. You're a huge, black, psychic suck hole."

"Let's pretend you're right. So what?"

Brian nods. "Exactly. Got any plans today?"

"Besides therapy and group? Not really."

"So your afternoon is free?"

"Pretty much."

"Meet me back here for lunch." He sweeps his tray off the table and walks away, leaving Lily gaping and disoriented.

§§§

I follow Brian through the long, white halls.

In his room, he switches on his tablet. The computer,

along with internet access, is a privilege he's earned by being on his best behavior for months. An organized sociopath, he finds it easy to toe the line in order to procure the necessary tools to achieve his first masterpiece: *Number One*.

He cracks his knuckles as he surfs the net. She's dangerous, and that is such a turn on. It also confounds him. Does he want to date her or kill her?

First, he wants to date her. Later, he can kill her.

viii

As I watch Brian gaze at his reflection in the mirror, I lose faith in his ability to end Lily's life. He's in love with her.

My fascination with her life at Careview, and Brian's interest in her, has distracted me. I need to get back on track. *Psst.* The head of Brian's shadow turns in my direction. *Can you hear me?* I ask.

It nods. A slight, but definite nod!

I hardly know what to say next. *Have you ever acted independently of your host?*

No. This is a first. While Brian continues to stare at himself in the mirror, his shadow swivels its head from side to side. *Teach me to do more!*

I'm thrilled. Assuming his existence has been as miserable as mine, I hastily reply, *Of course! It must be dreadful being the shadow of someone whose only dream in life is to become a serial killer.*

It has its moments.

I confide the source of my power: a compelling desire to do good in the world.

Good is so subjective.

Perhaps, but justice isn't. I tell Brian's shadow about Charlene and Trey.

It fixates on Trey. *They had sex at school?*

Yes.

In his car?

Yes. Lily did it wherever he wanted.

The shadow shakes it head. *I had no idea she was such a slut.*

Who cares about that? I ask.

Brian thinks she's a virgin.

How did I miss the day she told that whopper? *Is that what she told him?*

Not in so many words.

§ § §

Brian studies Lily from a distance. Ensconced in the most comfortable chair in the recreation room, she's holding court.

A loose group of patients form a ragged circumference around her. It's mostly females waiting to place their orders. One at a time, the girls take a seat in the wooden chair opposite Lily. She scratches on a pad of paper—an inventory of their requests. As soon as one patient wanders off, another one takes her place.

Under Brian's tutelage, Lily's adjustment to the Careview environment has been remarkable. Her little black market thrives.

Once a month, the Danes show up at the hospital with wary hope and full shopping bags. Although their daughter has earned the privilege to personalize her attire, she eschews the makeup and jewelry other female patients enjoy wearing and trading.

But she does drive a mean bargain.

Her latest acquisition, a prized Rasta tam, hides her golden hair. The look suits her bare face, oversized work shirt, ripped jeans, and hemp slip-on shoes with crushed heels.

Brian crosses and uncrosses his arm in rhythm to his thoughts. He's written her poems, brought her flowers from the gardens, and made her gifts in their craft therapy sessions.

She remains as cold as ice.

He ponders his next overture.

Why do you put her on a pedestal when she won't even put out for you?

She lets him hold her hand, brush her hair, and hand-feed her dessert after dinner.

Does he really want to fuck her?

The thought of polluting their perfect union with base

lust troubles him. He prefers Lily pure and ethereal. His dark angel. Untouched.

Why did she have to fuck Trey?

Everywhere.

§§§

A few days later, I corner Brian and his shadow in the laundry room. *I thought he was ready to turn his fantasies into reality.*

He is.

Then why doesn't he just kill her? I ask.

He's obsessive. Everything has to be perfect.

What a perfect excuse to never take action. *He's not going to do it, is he?*

The anticipation is like a drug for him. He's still getting high on it.

Don't you want your freedom? I prod.

Yes. Brian's shadow disengages from Brian's body. It lurches in my direction. *I feel compelled to help you*, it whispers. I can barely hear it. *I want to put you out of your misery.*

Something is off. Just like me, it's a darker version of its host. However, unlike me, it grows weaker with every step it takes away from him. It doubles over. It's going to die! I rush to help it. *You need to reconnect!* Its weightlessness makes it easy for me to guide it back to its host.

I'm not as strong as you, it wheezes.

Help me achieve justice for Charlene Vale and you will be! How to move things along? My thoughts keep returning to a suicide pact. I explain to Brian's shadow how I urged Lily to use the knife in the Dane kitchen. *If her mother hadn't stopped her, Lily would be dead.*

Brian's shadow absorbs my tale. *And Brian would never have met her or fallen in love.*

Does he really love her? I ask.

She doesn't love him, does she?

It's nothing personal. Lily is incapable of love.

He's a fool.

The world will be a better place when they're both gone,

I say.

§§§

November first. *Dio de los Muertos.* The Day of the Dead.

People across the globe gather at cemeteries to pray for their loved ones. It's the perfect day to seize justice for Charlene and her unborn child.

A small, overgrown cemetery hides on the southern edge of the Careview Estate. Brian's shadow and I have insured our hosts are aware of its existence. After group therapy, they intend to sneak there to picnic among the moss-covered tombstones.

A couple of sheets and a stolen XACTO knife are packed in Brian's messenger bag. He meets Lily early for lunch in the dining hall, where they stuff the same bag and their pockets with slices of bread, cubes of cheese, an assortment of bruised fruit, and several cartons of chocolate milk.

Brian has traded one of Lily's iPod Nanos to a guard for extra grounds privileges. She requested a dozen from her parents—inventory for her brisk business. You'd think

93

they'd balk at the number, but they never ask any questions.

Lily, Brian, his shadow, and I traipse along the far wall that forms a perimeter around the grounds. By the time we reach our destination, Brian and Lily are damp with sweat.

A maple tree, flaming with the red of turned leaves, stands in the cemetery's center—a divine symbol, a cosmic blessing of our plan.

What a lovely day to die.

Brian, torn between equally strong urges to worship, violate, and kill his deified beloved, pops a chunk of apple between her parted lips. "Lily."

"Mmm."

"I've brought two sheets." He pulls them from his bag.

Lily's gaze hardens. "How many times do I have to tell you? I'm not going to have sex with you." She has no desire of her own, and sexual favors aren't necessary to manipulate him.

"I don't want to have sex," he assures her.

Her glare softens.

"I want us to go out together," he says.

This time her entire body tenses. "Go out where?"

"Of this life."

How romantic, I whisper into her mind.

She swats the side of her head.

You have nothing to live for. Why not go out like a comet? Be dramatic. Everyone will remember you and forget—

"Charlene Vale and her stupid fetus."

"What?" Brian asks.

Lily rises to her knees and reaches for him.

He takes her hands and holds them tight.

"Everyone is always talking about Char," Lily says. "As if she's some saint, when all she managed to do was get pregnant in high school and slam her car into a tree. It's not like she won a Nobel Prize or discovered the cure for Ebola. But if we do this, no one will remember her anymore. They'll remember me."

Yes. Yes, I encourage my beast. This one final act will

eradicate even the memory of Charlene Vale.

"It's ingenious." Lily watches Brian shred each sheet into ten lengths. "My parents will be devastated. It serves them right. They should never have locked me up in here."

That's right, Lily. Your suicide will haunt them forever.

Contemplating Spencer's and Blair's despair excites her. She helps Brian braid the strips into two sturdy ropes.

"I bet the story will go viral," he says. "They'll shut Careview down." Brian tosses both the modified sheets over a single stout limb, and then tests each one with his weight. Satisfied they can withstand the job, he circles one of the makeshift cords around Lily's neck like a garland. He takes his time executing an intricate, yet bulky, knot.

Do it now, his shadow whispers.

Lily reaches for the second line of sheets.

Before she can touch them, Brian yanks hard on her noose. His eyes gleam as her body bursts into the sky, swinging as though it's a mad pendulum. He watches with an expression of devotion as she kicks and claws at the taut rope of sheet. His beloved will die pure, never again to be tainted by the touch of another.

Lily's frozen expression is one of horror.

Brian's heart swells with tender emotion before the moment passes.

When he releases his hold on Lily's snare, her corpse thuds gracelessly against the ground.

His shadow applauds. *Number One.*

What the hell?

Brian spins on his heels and glowers in my direction.

Can he see me?

I take a step back.

"I knew it." He lunges in my direction.

Before I can run, he's squeezing my hand.

I gaze down. It has become flesh. My hand is attached to my arm which extends from my torso. I am entirely corporeal.

His eyes gleam. "You're Lily's shadow."

"You murdered her!" I say aloud.

"Are you going to tell on me?" He explodes into maniacal laughter.

What have I done?

The sound of Brian's glee dies away. He wipes his eyes. "What a rush."

I edge away from him.

"Don't you want some lunch?" he asks.

"Not hungry."

He clamps his hand on my shoulder. "You wanted me kill her, so at least thank me before you go." His fingers dig deep, separating muscle from bone.

"Thank you," I whisper.

"That's better." He lets go. "But I shouldn't have had to ask!"

This act of crossing the line between fantasy and reality has altered him.

"Should I kill her too?" he asks.

I scan the clearing. We're still alone. He wets his lips.

Not today, his shadow answers. *You've committed the*

perfect crime. Don't ruin it.

Brian cocks his head to the side, listening. I follow his gaze to Lily's corpse. "Right," he says. He retrieves an envelope from his bag. As he approaches the body, his fingers palpate the thick, linen paper engraved with his initials. He pulls the X-ACTO knife from his pocket and cuts a swatch of Lily's golden hair.

The souvenir is reverently sealed within the packet.

Perfect, his shadow says. *Now, bury the evidence.*

I turn and run, only stopping when I'm sure he's not following me. I heave bile into a bed of dormant greenery. The aftereffect of my metamorphosis, or my bitter reaction to witnessing a murder? Lily's death isn't even close to the victory I dreamed of.

Perhaps because I'm fully human.

Inside her room, I study myself in the mirror. My eyes are the color of espresso, not her crystal blue. I rip the striped tam from my head. A curtain of chocolate-colored hair falls around my shoulders..

I sag onto Lily's bed—my bed—absorbing the awful

miracle.

I am Lily Dane.

§§§

I've got to come up with some explanation for my physical transformation, something believable, so I can get out of Careview, and far away from Brian and his shadow.

I chew on my thumbnail.

With the privileges I've earned to personalize my appearance, and all the money my parents sink into this place, surely I can sell colored contacts and hair dye?

But why?

Dr. Felton will demand a reason.

For now, I tuck my hair back into Lily's crocheted hat and drift over to the small, unbreakable window.

The sky is three distinct lines of lavender, red, and orange.

I dig through Lily's drawers for one of those iPods. Rolling an earbud between my thumb and forefinger triggers a memory of Daisy Wright. Another layer of melancholy wraps around me. I return to the sunset, hoping she's out there, somewhere, singing her heart out.

Then I crank up the volume and dance for Charlene Vale and her unborn child.

November first. *Dio de los Muertos*. The Day of the Dead.

A smile of peace flickers across my face.

§§§

At first, Blair and Spencer believe that dying my golden hair the color of a raven's wing is another symptom of my descent into insanity, but as the reports from Careview became increasingly positive, everyone agrees it's a small concession to make for my recovery.

"Your daughter possesses an extremely sensitive nature, and the death of her best friend traumatized her," Dr. Felton explains. "Through dying her hair and insisting on wearing those colored contact lenses, she's created an alternate identity for herself. One that has the capacity to fully grieve the loss of her friend. It's quite a creative resolution."

I listen without feeling the need to interject.

Whatever the doctor needs to believe works for me, because as long as I'm within reach of Brian and his shadow, I'm at risk of becoming *Number Two*.

"You sure she won't try to harm herself again?" Blair asks.

"Lily's inner life was restricted when her friend died. By enlarging it, she's developed the capacity to embrace life's most extreme ups and downs. Not only has she developed excellent self-care skills, but she also now exhibits an impressive level of empathy for our other patients. I don't know a single one of them who won't be disappointed when she's discharged. She's become a veritable ray of sunshine here at Careview."

His effusive compliments make me blush.

I flop the loose heel of my shoe against the floor and pray they'll release me soon.

§§§

Three months later, I walk out Careview's front door.

Brian Lassiter remains a patient there. His insistence that he murdered Lily Dane got him removed from general population.

Last I heard, they upped his meds. He and his shadow are going to be locked away for a good, long time.

I don't understand everything about my own existence, but recently I've noticed a faint charcoal glimmer to my side when I stand in direct sunlight.

It's a kind of a happy ending.

The beast is dead, and I am very much alive.

Author's Note

In 2014, I had the idea to write a horrific fairy tale for Halloween. After searching for an original tale that might translate into something darker, I stumbled upon Hans Christian Andersen's "The Shadow". It was one of those obscure tales I was unfamiliar with, but the concept intrigued me.

A man who is a scholar moves from a cold country to a hot country where his shadow seems to shrink during the day and recover its form at night. In an apartment across the street, the life of an unseen stranger intrigues the scholar. One night, the man notices his shadow—cast in light from the other apartment—is the only visible presence across the way. Jokingly, he tells his shadow to explore the mysterious residence. The next morning his shadow is gone.

Years later, the man's shadow returns, well-dressed, well-traveled, and worldly. The shadow extracts a promise from the scholar to never reveal the secret of his identity. As years pass, the shadow leaves and returns, always inviting the scholar to travel with him. The scholar refuses until he is old and withered. Finally, the man agrees to travel with his shadow to a watering place (a place of healing) where they meet a princess who "sees things too clearly." The princess recognizes the shadow as someone who "can't cast a shadow". However, he strikes her as someone who is as unusual as he is wise, and she falls in love with him. She invites him to become her consort. The shadow asks the man to continue their ruse, but the scholar threatens to reveal the truth about the shadow's identity to the princess.

Before their wedding, the shadow manipulates the man's death.

A bit gruesome, but the perfect fairy tale to reshape into a horrific one.

I twisted the tale as follows: The male scholar becomes a young female. While the human is the innocent in the original, in my retelling the shadow is the innocent. Also in the original, it seems relatively easy for the shadow to separate from its host. I made the separation a central struggle of the tale. Rather than traveling to "a watering place", Lily travels to Careview Psychiatric Hospital for Challenged Teens, and rather than meeting a prince, she meets the wanna-be serial killer, Brian, who falls in love with her—or at least becomes obsessed with her.

Of course, there is a death in the end...but it isn't the shadow's!

As often happens along the way, details rearranged themselves, and the focal day of the story shifted from Halloween (October 31st) to Dio De Los Muertos

(November 1st).

Years ago, when I lived in El Paso, Texas, I fell in love with many things: the desert, the moon hanging over the Franklin Mountains, the abundance of roses, and the view of Mexico while driving I-10 to work every morning. But one of the things I carried with me when I left was the celebration of Dio De Los Muertos. From the moment I saw the colorful art in curio shops in the mall and my friends' homes, I was intrigued by a day to honor the dead. I'd already lost my mother and three grandparents. To discover there was a heritage of celebrating the dearly departed with festivals, food, music, dance, and vividly painted skulls and crafts, drowning in flowers, heartened and revivified me. Honoring the dead, celebrating their life, and being grateful they were part of mine made for a meaningful experience.

There are numinous moments to be found in grief, and I wanted to imbue the fleeting glimpse of that light in this retelling.

Thank You

I appreciate you spending your valuable time reading *I Am Lily Dane*. If you'd like to share the story with other readers, please tell a friend, or post a review on any book-ish site.

I'd also like to invite you to sign up for my newsletter: http://eepurl.com/wWKUj. It's quirky—like me:D—and I confess, it comes out sporadically, but I send a variety of things, including some (hopefully) pleasant surprises along with updates on all my new releases.

Sincerely,

First Chapter of The Tree Hugger

Mags

The fire's flames leap into the night sky like hope.

I'm settled on a log, with Ma on one side of me and

Graham on the other. Me and Graham are seven years old. Graham's Pa is on the other side of him. They're both sad inside cause Graham's ma died. Being sad inside is something I know about, so I never repeat things like: She's in a better place, or Just be happy you had the time with her that you did. Sometimes it's better to just sit quiet with a person. Sometimes that's all they need to keep the black hole of grief madness at a distance.

"There wouldn't be a single dictator in the world, cause everyone on the planet would have the right to defend themselves and the ones they love. Every community would grow their own vegetable gardens and have enough acres for grazing livestock. We don't need much meat, just enough to fit in the center of our palm each day." Ma holds out her hand in the firelight.

I gaze at her long, slim fingers that look so much like mine. I lean against her, and that hand comes around my back and squeezes my shoulder. I shut my eyes so I can take in the comfort of her touch. I let her voice seep in, too.

"And there would be plenty of butter to kill the cancer cells that's always mutating inside of us. Pfff. Margarine cain't do that. Plus, with everyone eating enough fat, their brains would work right. Who knows what the human race would be capable of if every person's brain worked at optimum? We could probly harness energy that wouldn't pollute the air we breathe or water we drink."

Ma's words become a lullaby, and before I know it, she's shaking me awake.

The night is cold now the fire's out.

Ma's got a jar in her hand. It's filled with fruit preserves, or soap, or some other luxury in short supply these days. She won the contest again. She always does. Her version of Utopia is always the best.

Around us, everyone is clearing out. Ma kneels down, and I crawl up on her back. We head home with Graham and his Pa walking beside us.

They say goodnight when we reach the fork in the dirt road.

§§§

Ma ain't really my mother; she's my grandmother. But my mother is gone. She left on a mission to the incorporated territory two years ago, and hasn't come back.

Everyone calls my grandmother Ma, so I do, too. Big Ma was her mother. We call my mother Little Mother, on account of her having me when she was so young—sixteen.

Things have changed a lot in the generation since the incorporation.

Ma had Little Mother when she was 31. Now, cause of the situation with the food supply, and the ongoing skirmishes with the Kyintans and the drug cartels, women are encouraged to birth early. The babies are healthier, and have a better chance at life.

Ma was born down south. She said it made her physically ache to leave her homeland. Like the deepest part of her soul was being wrenched away with every step north she took. She gets real sad when she tells me this, like the wound is fresh, even though it's been nigh on thirty years.

Little Mother and me was born right here in the Free Territories. Ma says that's life going on as life does.

Often enough, Ma reminisces about the day I was born. It makes me feel real good, not just like I'm loved, but like I'm wanted. It almost makes up for Little Mother leaving me behind.

"When you was born," Ma says, "you pressed your fists tight up against your chest, with your fingers curled, so they hid inside. And then you folded your knees up to your belly, so we had to hunt for your toes."

After she says that, I clench my fingers around my thumbs, and press my knuckles against my heart. It's kinda sign language for, "You and Little Mother is precious to me, too." Although more and more I'm not right sure Little Mother is precious to me.

Every few months, a hardened circuit rider reaches our settlement with bleak news and a handful of letters. I always hope there's one for me. There never has been. I never say nothing, just stuff the sadness down into the black hole Little Mother left inside me. Every day, it grows a little bigger.

"And your skin was so pale—unusual for a newborn, cause most times their skin is a patch of red blotches." Ma taps her lip. "But not yours. No, you looked just like a magnolia bud from the first moment. Those trees are ancient, and their buds are so tough." She crouches down to run two weathered fingers real soft against my cheek. "But their petals are creamy to the touch." Then she gives me a whopping smile. "Hain't ever been able to get one of those trees to grow up here, but I got my Mags."

She grabs me and squeezes me so tight, it feels like I'm gonna break in two. I squeal and squirm as she plasters me with sloppy kisses.

That's our ritual.

And my name is Magnolia, but everyone calls me Mags.

Graham

I reckon I've loved Magnolia from the moment I saw her. Except I cain't rightly remember when that was, on account of I was so young. Something about her dark green eyes, pale white skin, and cocoa-brown hair draws me to her. She's the shade under a tree on a high summer day, when your face gets burnt just crossing the yard. I'm the best friend she's got. Though I confess that's not saying much, since I'm the only friend she's got. Mags ain't really friendly. I don't blame her. A lot of folks think she's lazy on account of she can stay quiet and still for so long. But she ain't lazy, she's just real thoughtful and deep.

One morning, when Mags and I are almost nine years old, we sneak away from the settlement. She likes getting away from folks. It calms her almost as much as the quiet of dawn; Mags never misses a sunrise.

After we go a good distance, we reach an open field, and stretch out in the long grass. Even though neither of us says much, it's nice being with her. It always is.

After we've been lying there for almost half-the-day, I peek sideways.

She feels my eyes on her and twists to her side. A smile softens her face, and those big green eyes sparkle.

Even though Mags is prickly, there's something about her that's hard not to notice. From time to time I catch other boys in our settlement staring at her. It makes me feel protective. Maybe jealous, too. Today I want to know if she feels what I do: We got a connection that others don't share. But I ain't sure how to ask her. Maybe roundabout. "I know I'm not the best looking boy in our settlement," I begin.

She props herself up on her elbow, like she's real interested in what I got to say.

So I go on. "I'm also not the smartest or the strongest." My heart sinks a touch when she doesn't argue my points, but I'm halfway across the river. If I don't keep swimming, I'm gonna get swept away in the current. My gaze settles on my long legs. "But I reckon, one day, I'm gonna be the tallest."

An affectionate giggle spills outta her mouth. The tight band squeezing my chest loosens. She rolls onto her back. We stare at the clouds floating by. I try to figure out what to say next, but I'm stumped.

"Graham, none of that other stuff matters."

Her announcement stops my mind's churning for more words.

"Cause you got a right true heart, and a right true heart is the thing in this world that's got the most value."

I relax back in the grass. The rest of the afternoon we don't talk much. We don't need to.

My Pa says being quiet and comfortable in another person's presence is proof of companionability.

Mags and I is definitely companionable.

Mags

"Hush, Mags." Ma wraps her arm around my shoulders and pulls me to her. "Don't say nothing." She crouches down until her chin rests on the top of my head. My heart thumps in my chest, a biological GPS thudding a relentless, We right here. I'm sure whoever or whatever is out there can hear it.

Over my deafening pulse, I hear Ma sniff.

Gasoline.

Then I hear the glug-glug-glug of the fuel being poured. Ma's arm eases off my shoulder. I glance sideways and see her rise and point toward the brush.

She mouths, "River," and pushes the air with her hands.

I don't wait. I turn and run. I cain't hear her tread, but Ma can move through her forest quieter than anyone or anything that lives there.

I reach the steep bank and slip into the water as noiselessly as possible When I surface, Ma don't. "Ma?"

At first I just whisper, and swish my hands beneath the water, searching. She was right behind me. "Ma, where are you?" My heart cracks open like an egg. Black yolk spills out. My voice pitches higher as I grope the river. My hands remain stubbornly empty, and my thrashing sounds like it's being blasted through some rickety PA system. I need to calm down. Ma won't approve if I drown.

Maybe she's done some scouting and will join me quick. I stretch my toes, but still cain't touch bottom. I peer behind me. I'm treading water in the river's deep center. I kick out my legs, soft and quiet, and butterfly to the river's south bank.

When I can curl my toes in the muddy sand, I crouch, willing Ma to join me.

But she don't.

The first explosion cracks my ears hard. Putrid brown-black flames crest in the sky. Ma's forest pops and crackles—a mountain-size version of a campfire.

For a second I hearken back to sitting around the warm, orange glow at night.

But this morning, a chorus of sadness wails from the flames like a mighty ghost. A supernatural terror sweeps through me, is the best way I can explain it. There's no words, and there's no tune; only a song of despair raining down upon me like a storm.

I'm never gonna feel joy around a fire again.

An even bigger explosion rocks the ground.

Heat blankets my face. I'm sure my skin is on fire, but it's only my heart, scorching with terror for Ma.

The high-pitched squeals of pigs, and the smell of their burnt flesh add to the gruesome mix. Last week, three sows farrowed. Those poor piglets.

I smash the backs of my hands against the river's surface, my legs paralyzed. If Ma walks outta that inferno —crisp like the bark on the black walnut trees—she's gonna need help—medicine and bandages and such. And she'll wanna see me first thing. She'll wanna know I'm safe.

Ma's whip smart. Maybe she ain't on fire.

Then I remember the irrigation ditches. I pull myself

outta the river and tear alongside the water in the direction of the flames. I get a bad stitch in my side and have to push my hand against my abdomen so I can keep up my pace. When I see the pulleys and chains that operate the gate to the reservoir, hope explodes in my head. I'm gonna save Ma, and her forest, and them pigs. She's gonna be so damn proud. Probly tell stories round the campfire for years about how her little Mags was a hero the day the incorporators dared set fire to her woods.

Ma's outraged voice fills my head: Can you believe it? They went after my trees!

But the rusted metal of the pulleys ain't easy to yank. In a part of the country where rain is plentiful, the mechanism is a back-up measure: the least used part of the settlement's emergency relief program.

I grab the rusty links and pull with every ounce of my body. Barely a creak. I step back five feet, ten feet, and give myself a running head start and leap. My chest slams against the stubborn chains, and for an instant, the smell of iron hits my senses. The lever shifts about an inch-and-a-half. I repeat launching myself at the metal ropes again and again. Finally, the lever swings back, and the gate rises enough for stagnant water to rush down the gullies Ma ordered dug years ago, before I was even born. Maybe even before Little Mother was born.

I cry out, watching the water gush toward the fire. To stay clear of the ever-thickening smoke, I get down on my belly and wiggle alongside the growing stream. I head straight for the destruction.

The rescue folks from our settlement is on their way. Shouts ring out, but I ain't about to wait for em.

I gotta find Ma right now.

Soot and ash thicken the air. Even down low, I can hardly breathe or see. I keep twisting my hips, pushing off with my toes, and clawing with my fingers, certain any minute I'll see Ma emerge from the black haze, like some movie superhero we watch in the community building theater. Ma's style is military, with guns and knives and magazines crisscrossed over her chest. She wears boots and camouflage, and winds her long gray hair in a single braid, pinned tight at the nape of her neck. No jewelry or makeup. But she's the most beautiful woman in the settlement, with her leaf-green eyes and bark-tanned skin. And she's supple, moving like a sapling swaying in the wind.

When the heat gets too much, I make myself stand. Giving no heed to safety, I race around the burn site, bug-eyed. I figure the arsonists have already fled, cause I don't come across no one, even when I scream Ma's name until my lungs hurt and my throat feels raw.

§ § §

When I wake up in my own bed, Da's hovering over me. I struggle to raise my head. "How'd I get here?" Every word makes my throat bleed, at least that's what it feels like. I rub my neck, although it don't soothe anything.

"The rescue found you, on fire with the delirium," he says. "Ole Man tried to give you some lemon balm to chew on, and you almost took his finger off."

I'm trying to piece together what happened before the world turned black. "Why ain't you at the shop?" Da is the village butcher.

"Need to watch over my little girl."

The softness in his voice sets me on edge. Da's a lot of things; tender ain't one of them. "Where's Ma?"

He pushes the hair from my forehead with rough fingers. "She's gone."

I'm having a baby and it's name is Dread. "Where?"

He turns his face up to the tin ceiling.

Silent sobs rack my body. That baby I just had is wailing, and I don't think I'm gonna make it.

"Now, now, little girl."

I struggle to sit up. Da helps me. "I'm gonna be sick."

He gets the bucket and rubs my back, but only a stream of white and yellow spittle chokes from my lips. I settle back down in bed.

"Let me get Franny," he says. "She can make you some of her fine ginger tea. We need to start getting some nourishment back in ya."

I roll over and stare at the rough-hewn logs that make up the walls of our cabin. All I can think as I hear him shuffle across the dirt floor is that those logs is dead—just like the trees in Ma's forest, just like Ma and all her pigs. I cover my head with a quilt Big Ma made, and let the tears wash through me like a river.

I'm eleven years old.

Graham

Mags is different after Ma dies. Worse. She don't laugh and stalks off whenever someone tries to be funny. It earns her all kinds of new names: Grumpy Butt, Frowny Freak, Stick-in-the-Mudhole.

I run as much interference for her as I can, and she seems to appreciate it, but she seeks out my company less and less. I understand. The wound cuts to the roots of her, and it will take more than one season to heal.

One night me and Pa are eating dinner. I wait until

we're almost done before I bring up the topic weighing on my mind. "Have you heard, Mag's Da is writing laws now?"

"Umhmm," Pa sops up the last bit of sausage grease with a heel of bread. "He ain't wasting no time. Giving speeches, too. 'It's morally wrong for a woman to go off on her own, and against her husband's approval, especially in these trying times.'" Pa snorts. "He always resented Little Mother's abandonment, blamed Ma for it. I guess he likes to think Little Mother would still be letting him order her around if Ma hadn't encouraged her ambitions to preach."

"But why is he writing laws? Why does he have to go and make 'spousal abandonment' a crime?" I ask.

"A weak man prefers controlling others to controlling himself. He wants this law passed so next time he marries, his wife cain't leave him."

"He's not gonna give up on it. He's going after the votes."

"Franny gonna help him?" he asks.

"Pretty sure."

"That's unfortunate," Pa says. "Franny's got a way of wheedling and whining that makes folks say 'yes' just to shut her up."

"I know. And I'm worried about how it's all gonna affect Mags. She don't like Franny. As long as Ma was alive, Franny left Mags alone."

"Ma was tough. Her death, and Mag's unapologetic sadness about it, makes everyone in the settlement feel vulnerable. Like death might come for em without a dark cloud warning or crack of thunder."

His words don't ease my mind in the least.

The day the law passes, the corners of Mags' lips bow down into an unyielding glower, "I'm never getting married," she says.

I don't doubt her for a minute. Mags don't lie. But my heart does ache, cause I've been dreaming about taking her for my bride for an awful long time.

About the Author

Heidi Garrett is the author of the *Daughter of Light* fantasy trilogy about a young half-faerie, half-mortal searching for her place in the Whole.

She's also the author of *Once Upon a Time Today*, a collection of modern fairy tale retellings for adults who have already left home. *The Magic Cupcake* series is paranormal romance trilogy she writes with Billie Limpin.

Heidi was born in Texas, and attempted to reside in as many cities in that state as possible. She made it to Houston, Lubbock, Austin, and El Paso. After spending a decade in southern California, she now lives in Eastern Washington state with her husband, their two cats, her laptop, and her Kindle. Being from the South, she often contemplates the magic of snow.

You can find Heidi on her blog.

www.ingramcontent.com/pod-product-compliance
Lightning Source LLC
Chambersburg PA
CBHW030537130626
46552CB00006B/2296